A B C D E F

G H I J K L

M N O P Q R

S T U V W X

Y Z

Published titles by Florenza are:

Adventurous Olivia's Alphabet Quest

Barry Bear's Very Best, Learning to Say No to Negative Influences

If…The Story of Faith Walker

There's No Place Like My Own Home

The Tail of Max the Mindless Dog, A Children's Book on Mindfulness

Welcome Home Daddy, Love, Lexi

Children's Books coming soon are:

Acornsville, Land of the Secret Seed Keepers

Adventurous Olivia's Numerical Quest

Amiri's Birthday Wish

Micah and Malik's Super Awesome Excellent Adventure

Oh, My Goodness, Look at this Big Mess

Two Bees in a Hive

When Life Gives Us Wind

Young Reader Chapter Books coming soon are:

Hoku to the Rescue

Two-Thirds is a Whole

For more information regarding Florenza's books, or to contact her to speak at your school or event,

please visit www.florenza.org.

Adventurous Olivia's Alphabet Quest

Address inquiries to Contact@florenza.org

eBook ISBN 978-1-941328-20-0
Softcover ISBN 978-1-941328-14-9
Hardcover ISBN 978-1-941328-19-4

Words to Ponder Publishing Company, LLC

Printed in the United States of America

For more information, visit https://www.florenza.org

ADVENTUROUS
OLIVIA'S
Alphabet Quest

By Florenza Denise Lee

Illustrated and Designed by Fx And Color Studio

DEDICATION PAGE

I dedicate this book to my family, Trefus, Jessica, and Missy for being my first and loudest cheerleaders. To Laurie Coleman, Natasha, Lauren, Olivia, and Taylor Beck for usage of your likenesses and names. I have thoroughly enjoyed writing these wonderful books in the Adventurous Olivia Book Series. Team Olivia all day!

Florenza

This Book Belongs To:

____

ALPHABET
QUEST

Hi, I'm Olivia. Mom calls me
"Adventurous Olivia!"

Ms. Blom, my teacher, challenged the class to find
three words that begin with each letter of the
alphabet; those who complete the assignment will
receive FREE passes to the zoo! I love the zoo; it is
my favorite place to visit! With your assistance,
I am certain I will finish the task.
I already have two words for each letter, but I'm
having difficulty finding the third. Can you help?
I hope so! Should you see something that begins
with the letter of the alphabet on the page,
do me a favor and SHOUT IT OUT!

Aa

"**ALL ABOARD!** Time to watch astronauts wearing aprons, eat almonds and apples!

Do you see another word that starts with the letter A? If so, shout it out!"

1. Aprons

2. Apples

3._______________

Bb

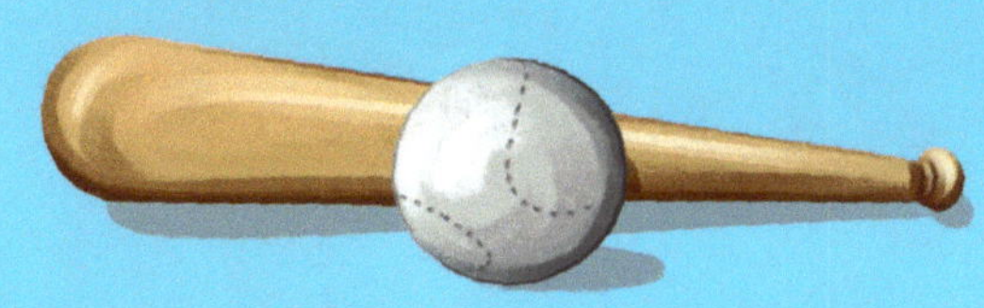

"BOUNCING BALLS AND BLOWING BUBBLES!

I found bagels and balloons for the letter B.

What other word do you have to complete

my list? Don't be shy, shout it out!"

1. Bagels

2. Balloons

3.________________

HAPPY BIRTHDAY
Happy Birthday!

Cc

"CAN'T COMPLAIN!

Nothing compares to cupcakes with candles; they are my favorite. Can you find another word that begins with the letter C?"

1. Cupcakes

2. Candles

3._________________

Dd

"**DON'T DABBLE, DAISY!** Time to get Daphne, my stuffed dolphin out of the dryer!

Don't delay! As soon as you discover another word beginning with the letter D, shout it out!"

1. Dryer

2. Dolphin

3.________________

Ee

"I'M EXAMINING EGGS in search of elephants, emus, and eagles! Can you think of another word that begins with the letter E?"

1. Elephants

2. Emus

3._______________________

Ff

"**WHILE PICKING FLOWERS** with Freddy Frog, a firetruck sounded like wee-woo, wee-woo, as it drove by! Can you think of another word that begins with the letter F?

That's fantastic!"

1. Freddy

2. Firetruck

3._______________

Gg

"**GANGWAY!** Goldie wants to see gorillas eating grapes on TV. Can you think of another word beginning with the letter G? Say it, and I will gladly jot it down!"

1. Grapes

2. Gorillas

3.________________

Hh

"HIP, HIP, HOORAY! Happiness is eating hamburgers with Henry, our hamster. Do you have a word that begins with the letter H! Just hearing you say it makes me happy!"

1. Hamburger

2. Henry

3._______________

Ii

"**IMAGINE** if igloos were made of ice cream instead of ice? Wouldn't that be incredible?

Can you think of another word that begins with the letter I?"

1. Igloos

2. Ice cream

3._______________

Jj

"JUMPING JOSEPHAT! My jigsaw puzzle is a picture of the jungle. What J word may I add to my list? Just shout it out, and I will jot it down!"

1. Jigsaw

2. Jungle

3._______________

Kk

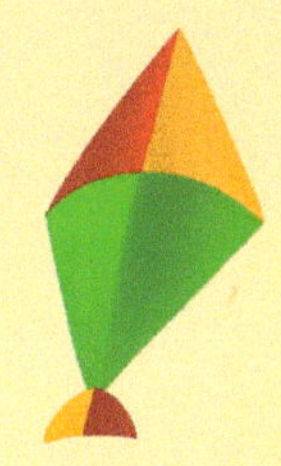

"**KEEP CALM KITTY!** You are so cute with your Koolie-Whip hat. Can you find another word that begins with the letter K?"

1. Kitty

2. Koolie-Whip

3._________________

Ll

"**LA-LA-LA!** I love the lyrics to the song, 'The lion wears lilac lipstick'! Take a good long look, can you spot something that begins with the letter L?"

1. lyrics

2. Lipstick

3.______________

MAP

Mm

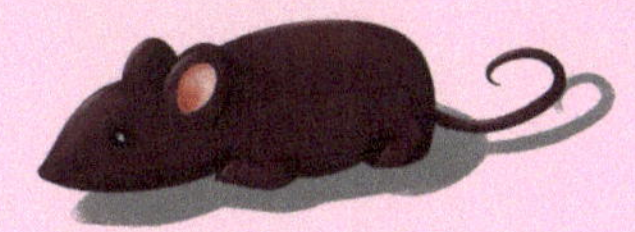

"MY GOODNESS, this is so much fun!

Wearing Mommy's makeup makes me look

marvelous in the mirror! Do you see a word

that begins with the letter M?"

1. Makeup

2. Mirror

3.___________________

NEWS
⁉

Nn

"NO NEED to panic, we have lots of napkins for Nana's nachos! Can you think of another word that begins with the letter N?"

1. Napkins

2. Nachos

3.___________________

Oo

"**OLIVER OCTOPUS** loves olives and oranges!

Can you think of another O word to add to

my list? Just shout it out!"

1. Olives

2. Oranges

3.___________________

Pp

"**PRETEND**, Peter Piper was a pirate whose pumpkin contains pickled peppers!

What other item do you see that begins with the letter P?

Wonderful! Let's proudly add it to the list!"

1. Pirate

2. Pumpkin

3._________________

Qq

"I'M QUEEN FOR THE DAY!

To enter, you must pass my quiz. Ready?

Set? Go! Quickly spell quartz then

shout out another word that begins

with the letter Q!"

1. Quiz

2. Quartz

3.__________________

Rr

"ROBBY THE ROBOT wears ribbons and red roses! What word may I add to my list for the letter R? Say it really loudly, I can't hear you over Robby's racket!"

1. Ribbons

2. Roses

3.________________

Ss

"**SALLY, SARA'S SISTER,** loves eating salad with a spoon while stumping up the stairs. What other word beginning with the letter S may I add to my list?"

1. Salad

2. Spoon

3.________________

T

Tt

"**TA-DA!!** Timothy, my pet turtle, loves to tiptoe on the table as I tap dance to the tunes. Do you have a word I may add for the letter T?"

1. Timothy

2. Table

3.________________

Uu

"**UNBELIEVABLE!** Eunice (who wears an umpire's uniform) taught me how to play the ukulele. Can you think of a unique word beginning with the letter U to add to the list?"

1. Ukulele

2. Uniforms

3._______________

Uv

"VROOM! VROOM! Vacate the premises! The volcano is erupting with veggies and volleyballs. Do you see another item that begins with the letter V? If so, shout it out!"

1. Volcano

2. Veggies

3._________________

Ww

"**WOWSERS!** While washing the windows, I saw a wasp waltzing with a walrus! What word beginning with the letter W did you find?"

1. Wasp

2. Walrus

3.____________________

Xerus
xebec
PRINT
X

Xx

"XAVIER the Xerus is riding a xebec!

Aren't you excited? Can you think of

another X word to add to the list?

Just two more letters to go!"

1. Xebec

2. Xerus

3.________________

YEAR 2019
YARD SALE

Yy

"**YESTERDAY,** Yolanda and I ate yogurt and played with our yoyos. Can you think of a Y word I may add to my list?"

1. Yolanda

2. Yogurt

3.____________________

Zz

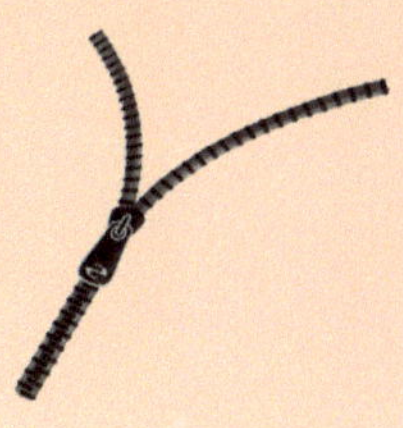

"ZENITH! I have zippers and zucchini! With your help, we will complete the list! Stand and shout out our last word, then it's off to the zoo we will go!"

1. Zippers

2. Zucchini

3.________________

ZOO
ZOO

"Thanks for your assistance. I couldn't

have completed my assignment without

your help. Be sure to think of new

exciting words each time you read

the book! Bye!"

ADVENTUROUS OLIVIA'S ALPHABET QUEST

Ms. Blom, Olivia's teacher, has given her a homework assignment to complete an alphabet list for free passes to the zoo. Olivia has two words that begin with each letter, but needs your assistance finding the third! When you see or hear a word that starts with the alphabet she is searching, SHOUT IT OUT! With your help, Olivia will be able to enjoy an afternoon with her family at the zoo!

ABOUT THE AUTHOR

Florenza is an author, publisher, narrative coach, speaker, radio talk show host, Master Storyteller, wife, and mother. Florenza and her husband, CSM (Ret US Army) Trefus Lee have been married for nearly 38 years and reside in Hampton, Virginia. Their daughters: Jessica and Missy call Honolulu, Hawaii home.